I, *Geronimo Stilton*, have a lot of mouse friends, but none as **spooky** as my friend CREEPELLA VON CACKLEFUR! She is an enchanting and MYSTERIOUS mouse with a pet bat named **Bitewing**. Creepella lives in a CEMETERY, sleeps in a marble **sarcophagus**, and drives a **hearse**. By night she is a special effects and set designer for SCARY FILMS, and by day she's studying to become a journalist! Her father, Boris von Cacklefur, runs the funeral home Fabumouse Funerals, and the von Cacklefur family owns the CREEPY Cacklefur Castle, which sits on top of a skull-shaped mountain in MYSTERIOUS VALLEY.

YIKES! I'm a real 'fraidy mouse, but even I think Creepella and her family are AWFULLY fascinating. I can't wait for you to read this fa-mouse-ly funny and SPECTACULARLY SPOOKY tale!

Geronimo Stilton

Creepella von Cacklefur

Bitewing

Billy Squeakspeare

Grandpa Frankenstein

An extremely mad scientist and an expert in Egyptian mummies.

A journalist who lives in Mysterious Valley and solves spooky cases with her inseparable pet bat, Bitewing.

A famous writer and friend of Creepella.

Shivereen

Grandma Crypt

Snip and Snap

Troublemaking twins and expert spies.

Creepella's favorite niece.

Dolores

Kafka

She loves spiders, and her pet is a gigantic tarantula named Dolores.

The von Cacklefur family's pet cockroach.

Booey the Poltergeist

The mischievous ghost who haunts Cacklefur Castle.

Boneham

The butler to the von Cacklefur family, and a snob right down to the tips of his whiskers.

Baby

He was adopted and raised with love by the von Cacklefurs.

Madame LaTomb

The family housekeeper. A ferocious were-canary nests in her hair.

Chef Stewrat

The cook at Cacklefur Castle. He dreams of creating the ultimate stew.

Boris von Cacklefur

Creepella's father, and the funeral director at Fabumouse Funerals.

Chompers

The von Cacklefur family's meat-eating guard plant.

AN EERIE
E-MAIL

I hurried home after a long day at work. I was so tired that my whiskers were **DROOPING**. All I wanted to do was relax in my favorite **comfy** chair.

Don't get me wrong — I wasn't planning on **STARING** at the walls all night. I had brought home some work to do. But I wanted to do it calmly, in peace and quiet. No **ringing** phones. No doors *slamming*. And no coworkers yelling at one another!

Sorry, I haven't introduced myself. My name is Stilton, *Geronimo Stilton*. I'm the publisher of *The Rodent's Gazette*, the most **FaMouse** newspaper on Mouse Island.

It was already late and I was as tired as a rat being chased by a cat. But I really wanted to write a nice article about the city I live in. I **love** my city!

I turned on my laptop and looked at **PHOTOS** of all the places, buildings, and statues that make **New Mouse City** a **FANTASTIC** place to live.

What a great city!

My sister, Thea, took all the photos. She's a special correspondent for the newspaper. I checked out **PHOTOS** of the port, City Hall, Singing Stone Square, the Statue of Limburger . . . and then I yawned. I was so **sleepy**!

I looked at the 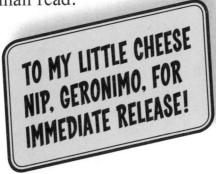 clock. It was ten fifteen!

"Time to hit the sack!" I exclaimed, *stretching.*

As I put on my pajamas, I remembered something — I hadn't checked my e-mail in hours. So I typed in my password and saw a new message pop up on my screen.

It was from my friend CREEPELLA VON CACKLEFUR! I turned as PALE as a slice of Swiss cheese. There is absolutely nothing relaxing about CREEPELLA.

The e-mail read:

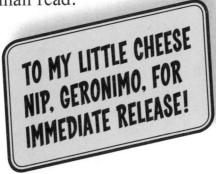

TO MY LITTLE CHEESE NIP, GERONIMO, FOR IMMEDIATE RELEASE!

There was a file attached. It was Creepella's latest novel. You might know that she lives in **Mysterious Valley**. All her books are about **CREEPY** creatures, like vampires, mummies, and monsters. They are **thrilling, chilling** tales!

My tail **twitched** in fright before I even read the first word. But I was very curious, so I opened the file. Then I read the book all the way through, and it was so good that I couldn't stop thinking about it! Soon the rays of the cheddar-**yellow** sun were peeking through my window.

"What a **STRANGE** story," I whispered.

Then the doorbell rang. I was **GROGGY** from not sleeping, and I stumbled to the door and opened it.

"Good morning, Uncle Geronimo. Are you ready yet?" It was **BENJAMIN**, my favorite nephew, with his friend **Bugsy Wugsy**. I had promised to have breakfast with them!  **"HOLEY CHEESE!** I'm late. Give me a second," I called as I ran into my room. I dressed so quickly that my heart was **pounding** like I was a mouse caught in a trap.

When I was done, I found Benjamin and Bugsy Wugsy looking at Creepella's story. They read it in no time.

"It's a strange story . . . but awesome!" they exclaimed.

"Do you **REALLY** think so?" I asked, straightening my tie.

"Absolutely!" Bugsy Wugsy replied.

"You have to publish it *IMMEDIATELY*, Uncle Geronimo!" Benjamin added.

I decided to take their advice. So I present to you now the amazing, breathtaking new story by Creepella von Cacklefur!

It's called:

The Return of the Vampire.

I hope you'll like it as much as Benjamin and Bugsy Wugsy did.

By the way, we went out for BREAKFAST that morning.

"What would you like?" asked the waitress.

We didn't think about it twice. We looked at one another. Then we all said our orders at the same time.

"A GLASS OF TOMATO JUICE!"

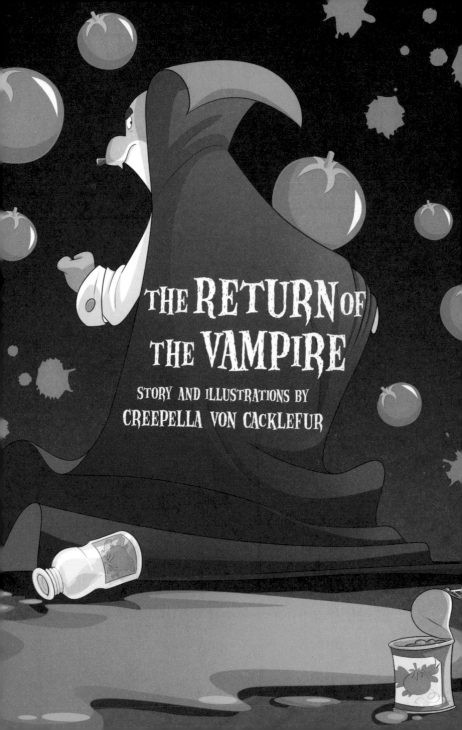

THE RETURN OF THE VAMPIRE

STORY AND ILLUSTRATIONS BY
CREEPELLA VON CACKLEFUR

THE LATE-NIGHT VISITOR

The clock struck midnight. The residents of Cacklefur Castle were **snoring** peacefully in their beds, dreaming deliciously **scary** nightmares, when . . .

DONG DONG DONG DONG DONG

The deep sound of a funeral bell broke the tomb-like silence in the **DARK** castle. Creepella von Cacklefur woke up with a start. The doorbell!

Her pet bat, **Bitewing**, was hanging **UPSIDE DOWN** from her bed canopy. He opened one eye, annoyed.

"It's probably just a dream," he said sleepily.

DONG DONG DONG DONG DONG

This time, Creepella jumped out of bed, put on a purple silk robe, and *hurried* out of the room.

Who could it be at this hour?

In the hall, she almost BUMPED into her niece, Shivereen.

"Who could it be, Auntie?" Shivereen asked with a yawn.

DONG DONG DONG

"I don't know, but this visitor is more persistent than a hungry MOSQUITO!" Creepella replied, running down the stairs.

The rest of the von Cacklefur family had already gathered in the Great Hall. Only Grandpa Frankenstein was missing. He was in his underground LABORATORY, working on one of his unusual new inventions. The middle of the NIGHT was his favorite time to work. But even without Grandpa Frankenstein there, the von Cacklefurs were still the most BIZARRE of all the

bizarre families in Mysterious Valley.

"It can't be a guest at this time of night!" exclaimed Boris von Cacklefur, **CREEPELLA'S** father. He wore his pajamas and a nightcap.

Boneham, the butler, was the only one not wearing wrinkled pajamas. He was dressed in his perfectly ironed UNIFORM.

"True," Boneham agreed. "This is a very inappropriate time for a courtesy call!"

Everyone stared at the DOOR. Creepella stepped forward, holding her breath.

Then she opened it. A strange SHADOW fell across the doorway.

The visitor wore a black cape with an enormouse collar. He had sharp fangs. There was no doubt: He was a **VAMPIRE**!

But he had such a sad look on his face that the von Cacklefurs weren't afraid. In fact, they felt sorry for this **CHEERLESS** creature.

"Please come in," Creepella said.

The vampire stepped inside. "I'm sorry, I don't mean to bother you," he mumbled timidly. "I was looking for . . . Does Professor Frankenstein live here?"

"Yes, he does," Creepella replied. She turned to Shivereen. "Please run and get Grandpa. I'm sure he's in his Think Tank."*

Shivereen raced off, and the von Cacklefurs waited in **silence**. Then Grandpa Frankenstein's voice boomed throughout the gloomy castle.

* Grandpa's laboratory. It's where he performs all his experiments!

"I hope you have a good reason for disturbing me!" he said grumpily. "I was making a new potion out of **MUMMY'S BREATH.**"

When he saw the late-night guest, he **froze** in place for a moment.

Then he ran toward the vampire and gave him a great big **HuG**.

"Well, rattle my bones! I can't believe my eyes. Is it really you?"

So wonderful to see you!

Is it really you?

VAMPIRE TROUBLES

Grandpa Frankenstein hugged the vampire again and then turned to his family.

"May I present **FRANCO FANGLEY**, an expert on tomato juice and an old friend!" he said proudly. "Oh, the **MISCHIEF** the two of us used to get into!"

The **SAD** look came over the vampire's face again. Grandpa Frankenstein **LOOKED** him over from his pointy fangs down to his pointy shoes.

"My friend, you look rather **GLOOMY**, and not your usual ghostly, ghastly self," he said. "What's wrong?"

FRANCO FANGLEY
VITAL FACTS

FIRST NAME: Franco

LAST NAME: Fangley

ADDRESS: Castle Marinara, located at the foot of Vampire Peak

PROFESSION: V.T.T.J.
(Vampire Taster of Tomato Juice)

APPEARANCE: Pale white fur and pointy teeth

UNUSUAL HABIT: Sleeps all day inside a coffin that once belonged to Count Ratula. Awakens at sunset.

WARDROBE:
Burgundy vest, white ruffled shirt, black velvet cape lined in crimson, with a large wide collar, pointy shoes made of shiny leather. This outfit gives him the look of a serious and refined gentlemouse.

CHILDHOOD: Made mischief with his best friend, Grandpa Frankenstein

FYI: Like all vampires, he can't stand garlic!

With a loud SIGH, Franco began his tale.

"Do you remember Castle Marinara, my home?" he asked.

"**Of course!**" Grandpa Frankenstein replied. "I'll never forget the splendid evenings we spent playing Steal the Tarantula in those **MOLDY** halls. Is the place still as **GLOOMY** as ever?"

Franco sniffled loudly. "It would be," he replied, "if it weren't infested by strange monsters and ghosts . . . *sniff*!"

Creepella's ears perked up. "What did you say? Monsters and ghosts in a vampire's castle? This would make an astounding article for *The Shivery News*. Maybe I could even get a new book out of it!"

"The only astounding thing about it is the

amount of *trouble* those *creatures* cause!" Franco exclaimed. "They play one PRANK after another on me. They fill my casket with bread crumbs. They spread cream cheese on the floor to make me slip. And yesterday they switched my tomato juice with bottles of garlic tea!"

Bread crumbs

Cream cheese

Creepella's trouble-making nephews, Snip and Snap, started taking notes. "Those are really AWESOME tricks!" they said.

Garlic tea

Hee hee!

"My castle is truly BEAUTIFUL," the vampire continued. "But if this goes on, I'll be forced to leave it. Can you help me?"

Creepella nodded. "You came to the right place. We von Cacklefurs always help those in need. We now have a new mission: SAVE THE VAMPIRE!"

"Can I be part of the mission, Auntie?" asked Shivereen.

"Of course!" Creepella replied. "You and Bitewing can be part of the team, along with Grandpa and me."

Grandma Crypt LOOKED concerned. "Dearest, don't forget to bring warm clothing," she told Creepella. "Castle Marinara

is in the mountains, and it **snows** a lot up there."

"I'll bring some," Creepella promised. She turned to her team. "Let's *gear up* and get going! We've got a vampire to save!"

"Well said, my dear granddaughter!" said Grandpa Frankenstein.

Then they all *rushed* off to pack for their mission.

MONSTERS, HERE WE COME!

Creepella bounded up the stairs leading to her room. Bitewing **flapped** his wings around her head, complaining all the way.

"Why do I have to come?" he whined. "I don't like the $COLD$ and I really hate snow!"

Creepella knew the best way to convince her pet bat to do something he didn't want to: She tossed him a piece of swamp-worm **candy**. He caught it and swallowed it in one gulp.

"Yummy! Fine! I'll go! I'll go! I'll go!" he screeched.

Creepella grinned and entered her room. "The first step in a MYSTERIOUS MISSION like ours is to get the right equipment!"

She opened up Wardrobe, the huge walking, talking cabinet that held her clothes and gave her fashion advice.

"Castle Marinara is at the foot of Vampire Peak, a very SNOWY mountain," declared Wardrobe. "Therefore, I suggest a coat of ram's WOOL. Dyed purple, of course."

Creepella put on the coat and combed her long hair, which was as black as midnight. Then she brushed the shimmering scales of a green lizard on her eyelids. Finally, she applied shiny lip gloss made from the drool of a Siberian toad. Her talking MIRROR gave her a compliment.

You look gorgeous!

Thank you!

"*You look gorgeous, Miss Creepella!*"

it said. "What's today's mission?"

"Save the **VAMPIRE**!" she replied.

Downstairs, she found the rest of the mission team waiting by the door. Grandpa Frankenstein was carrying a small **BAG**.

"What's in the bag?" asked Shivereen.

"This is my latest invention," he replied proudly. "The B.P.L.M."

"The B.P.L.M.?" Shivereen asked.

"The Bag of Pesky Little Monsters!" Grandpa Frankenstein explained. "Besides

Gorgo, many smaller **monsters** live in our moat."

Creepella nodded. "It's said that they all have special abilities, but no one has ever seen them."

"Until today!" chuckled Grandpa, **patting** the bag. "But never mind that. Let's get moving! Don't worry, you'll get to see them all at the right time!"

Let's get moving!

The team left the *CASTLE*. When Franco Fangley saw Creepella's car, the **Turborapid 3000**, he smiled for the first time since he had arrived.

Cacklefur Castle

"This is a magnificent hearse," said the vampire. "And I happen to be an expert on them!"

Vampire Peak is somewhere around here

Squeakspeare Mansion

"Thank you," said Creepella, and they piled into the purple car and **sped off**. After a few minutes on the road, Shivereen looked confused.

"Where are we going?" she asked. "This isn't the road that leads to Vampire Peak."

"Didn't I tell you?" Creepella answered. "First we're going to pick up my friend *Billy Squeakspeare*. He'll be very happy to go with us. A writer like him is always in search of interesting stories. Besides, he **loves** solving mysteries with me!"

BILLY-WILLY JOINS THE MISSION

Billy Squeakspeare couldn't fall asleep. As usual, the NOISY ghosts who lived in the mansion were keeping him AWAKE. Finally, he gave in, got dressed, and went into his office. Since he couldn't sleep, he decided he might as well answer some of his mail.

On the top of the pile of letters on his desk was a blue ENVELOPE. Inside was an ad for a snowy vacation.

I'm so sleepy!

Coming Soon!

Are the chills in Gloomeria not chilly enough for you? Try freezing your fur with a vacation in the snow!

SKIING! SNOWBOARDING! TUBING!

For further information, contact:
Stan Shadyfur
413 Swindle Street
Gloomeria

"A vacation in the snow is the **last** thing I need," Billy said. "What I really need is a *good night's sleep* without any ghosts!"

The doorbell rang.

"Who could it be at this hour?" Billy wondered with a **YAWN**.

He opened the door to see his friend Creepella, as **BRIGHT EYED** and bushy tailed as ever.

"Hi, Billy-Willy! You're already dressed!" she said cheerfully. "Good boy! We're just starting on an exciting mission!"

"Wh-what kind of MISSION?" Billy STUTTERED.

"You'll soon find out!" Creepella promised. Before he could protest, she wrapped a scarf around his neck and *pushed* him into the car. Billy found himself sitting next to a mouse he had never seen before.

"Glad to meet you," said Franco. "I'm Franco Fangley, VAMPIRE."

Poor Billy fainted on the spot.

"Oh, no, did I scare him?" Franco asked.

"Actually, Billy-Willy scares easily," Creepella explained.

Billy slowly opened his eyes and noticed some large stains on Franco's collar.

"Are those r-r-red spots . . . **B-B-BLOOD**?" asked a terrified Billy.

"Blood? No, of course not!" replied Franco. "It's fresh t🍅m&to juice. I am a V.T.T.J. of a very respectable level."

"A **V.T.T.J.** — of course," Billy said, nodding. Then he whispered to Bitewing, "Wh-what is th-that?"

Silly Billy!

No, it's tomato juice!

Is it b-blood?

"It's obviously a **V**ampire **T**aster of **T**omato **J**uice," replied the bat. "Didn't you know that, Silly Billy?"

"So tell us, my dear vampire," Creepella said "What kind of monsters and ghosts are **infesting** your home?"

"V-vampire? M-monsters? G-ghosts?" stammered Billy.

Then he **fainted** again.

THE
HAUNTED CASTLE

Franco started to tell his story. "A few months ago, I started hearing strange noises in the castle," he began.

Shivereen took a notebook out of her pocket and started taking notes.

"Then I saw scary-looking SHADOWS in every hallway," Franco went on. "And then the strange noises became horrific howls and shrieks!"

"What kind of howls?" Creepella asked. "Sad, like the cries of a lonely werewolf? Or are they more like the SHRIEKS of a hungry monster?"

"It's difficult to explain," replied Franco. "They sound sort of . . . metallic."

"Metallic shrieks. How unusual," remarked Creepella.

Billy opened his eyes again. "A-are we there yet?" he asked.

The Turborapid sped along the steep road that led to VAMPIRE PEAK, the tallest mountain in Mysterious Valley. Creepella stopped at the foot of the peak.

They all stepped out onto the snow-covered ground in front of Castle Marinara. Cheddar-yellow streaks of sunlight were beginning to appear in the dark sky.

Franco gasped. "I must go inside! If a RAY of sunlight touches me, I'm done for! I will see you all tonight."

The vampire quickly vanished inside the castle. The others stayed outside to admire the frosty towers of Castle Marinara.

"Those towers are fabumously FRIGHTENING," remarked Shivereen, pointing to the stone fangs that decorated them.

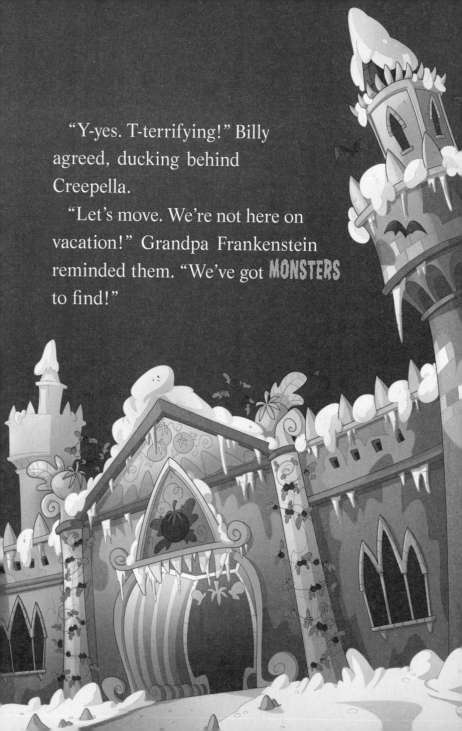

"Y-yes. T-terrifying!" Billy agreed, ducking behind Creepella.

"Let's move. We're not here on vacation!" Grandpa Frankenstein reminded them. "We've got MONSTERS to find!"

Inside the castle, the furniture was covered with COBWEBS and dust. They walked down a hallway lined with old suits of armor.

"How marvelous!" Creepella exclaimed. "Isn't it beautiful, Billy-Willy?"

"N-not exactly," stammered Billy, shivering with fright. "Why are all the curtains closed?"

"Because this is a vampire's castle, of course," answered Creepella. "No sunlight must enter at all."

"H-how about a l-lightbulb, then?" Billy suggested. He wasn't sure if he could stay another minute in the CREEPY, dark castle.

"I've got just what we need," said Grandpa Frankenstein, rummaging through his bag. "Meet

Hello, Glimmer!

Glimmer, the little monster that **glows** in the dark!"

He took a tiny green monster out of the bag. She opened her eyes, gave a little yawn, and then began to give off a soft yellow light that lit up the hallway.

Creepella clapped her hands. "Perfect, Grandpa. Now we . . . *EVERYBODY STOP!*" she cried suddenly.

"What is it? Monsters?" asked Grandpa Frankenstein.

"No, it's a clue," Creepella said. "I see some PAWPRINTS!"

THE SECRET PASSAGE

Creepella pointed to the floor, where small **square** pawprints could be seen on a thick layer of dust. The prints were very far apart.

"Wh-who do you think made those?" Billy asked.

"Franco wears **pointed** shoes, so they can't be his," Creepella said thoughtfully. "Also, monsters and ghosts don't leave pawprints. Just **SLIME** or **Ectoplasm**."

She took her cell phone from her pocket and flipped it open.

"Who are you calling?" asked Shivereen.

"Professor Cleverpaws, my former teacher," replied Creepella. "Besides being an expert in hiding places, she also specializes in **PAWPRINTS**, tracks, and general clues."

The phone rang twice and Professor Cleverpaws answered.

"**Helloooooooooooooooooo!**" she said cheerfully.

"Good morning, Professor. This is Creepella."

"My favorite pupil!" said the professor. "Are you involved in another **MYSTERY**? Tell me, is that adorable scaredy-mouse still working with you?"

Creepella glanced at the frightened Billy.

"Yes, he's here with me," she replied. "We're lending a paw to a **VAMPIRE** whose castle is haunted, and we found some very strange pawprints."

"Send me a **PHOTO** with your phone," Professor Cleverpaws instructed. "I'll take a look at them and get back to you as soon as I can."

"Thank you, Professor," Creepella said. "I knew I could count on you!"

She quickly snapped a photo and sent it off. Then the team continued to **EXPLORE** the castle. The hallway led to a marble **staircase**. They climbed it and found themselves in the **Portrait Gallery**. Paintings of Franco's **SPOOKY-LOOKING** ancestors hung on the walls.

"What **CHILLING** faces!" Shivereen said with admiration.

"Yes, **CO-CHILLING**," Billy agreed. In fact, his whole body was shivering with fear. He started to feel **faint** again and looked for someplace to sit.

But there wasn't a seat or bench in sight. Billy sighed and leaned against the wall. For support, he gripped a small metal **dragon's head** that stuck out from the wall.

"AAAAAAAAAAAAAHHH!"

It was a doorknob! The door began to **SPIN** around and around, taking Billy for a wild ride.

Everyone but Billy **BURST** out laughing at the sight of it. Finally, Creepella grabbed the knob and pulled it, and the door slowed to a stop.

CREEPELLA'S green eyes **gleamed** with excitement. "Billy-Willy, you found a

SECRET PASSAGE!" she cried. "But I can't see what's back there. Grandpa, please give us some light."

Grandpa Frankenstein held up Glimmer to light the way and stepped into the dark passage.

"There's a staircase here that goes **down**," he reported. "Follow me!"

"D-down there?" Billy stammered. "But there could be **M-MONSTERS**!"

"Oh, Billy," Creepella said. "You live in a mansion with thirteen ghosts. I'm sure you can handle a few monsters, can't you?"

"Honestly, I don't think so," Billy admitted.

"You're such a kidder," Creepella said. "Come on, let's go!"

IT'S A TRAPDOOR!

Creepella dragged Billy down the stairs. Glimmer's soft light cast **ghostly shadows** on the moss-covered walls. **ghostly shadows**

The stairs went **down** . . . and **down** . . . and **down**.

"D-don't these stairs ever end?" Billy asked, catching his breath.

"This is great exercise!" Creepella said. She took the bag from her grandfather and **TOSSED** it to Billy. "Here, carry this and you can work out your arm muscles, too."

Billy caught the heavy bag and **LUGGED** it down the stairs with a groan.

"Too much for you, Billy?"
Grandpa Frankenstein asked.
"Because I feel FANTASTIC!
I've got more energy than a lightning
storm! Just look at this!"

He JUMPED down the last few stairs.
His paws made a strange sound when they
hit the floor.

Bonnnnnnnnnng!

"What an unusual sound! What did you hit, Grandpa?" Creepella asked.

He aimed Glimmer's light on the floor beneath him.

"Well, rattle my bones!" he exclaimed. "It's a TRAPDOOR made of iron!"

"There's a plaque on it," Shivereen said. She read it out loud.

**SECRET TRAPDOOR
TO THE SECRET ROOM
OFF THE SECRET PASSAGE.
DO NOT ENTER!
IT MUST REMAIN A SECRET!**

"I'm sure these secrets hold the key to our mystery," said Creepella. "We must open the door *immediately*!"

Billy shook his head doubtfully. "It won't be easy. Look at it! There's a **HEAVY** iron **CHAIN** keeping the door shut."

Grandpa Frankenstein chuckled. "A heavy chain? No problem!" He looked at Billy. "Please open my bag."

Billy obeyed, and Grandpa Frankenstein

took out another little monster. This one had a long head and lots of very SHARP teeth.

"This is CHOPPER, my favorite little MONSTER," Grandpa said. "There's nothing he can't cut with his sharp teeth."

He led the monster to the chain. Chopper chomped down, breaking the chain completely in half.

THE SECRETS OF THE SECRET ROOM

The smells of **MOLD** and **MILDEW** floated out from under the trapdoor. Glimmer's light revealed a small, **dark** room below.

"C-Creepella, I think I'll wait for you here," Billy said, taking a step back. "There must be a reason why there was a ch-chain on that door."

Creepella took the bag of monsters from him. "Fine, Billy, as long as you don't mind being all **ALONE** up here."

She headed down into the room, followed by Shivereen, Bitewing, and her grandfather. Billy looked around **nervously** and then hurried after them.

Grandpa Frankenstein lit up the **dark** room with Glimmer's light. It shined on a pile of objects in the corner. Shivereen took notes as Creepella described them.

"There's an old gramophone and some records. I see a movie projector, a long **MOLDY** sheet, and a wooden trunk. But it's **LOCKED.**"

Creepella tugged on the lock.

"Grandpa, can we use —"

"**CHOPPER?** Of course!" the mad scientist replied.

He removed Chopper from the bag, and the little monster started **chewing** on the lock.

CHOMP!

Nothing happened. The lock was too strong for Chopper's teeth.

"Rattle my bones! That's odd!" exclaimed Grandpa Frankenstein.

"I can smell the stench of **MYSTERY** coming from that trunk!" Creepella said, excited. "We *absolutely* have to open it!"

Her grandfather shook his head. "I know a way to open it, but it could be **DANGEROUS**," he said. "Perhaps we should just walk away from it."

"We can't **GIVE UP** now!" Creepella insisted. "Franco is counting on us!"

"Fine, but don't say I didn't warn you," Grandpa said. "All right, everyone. **Step back!**"

He took a small box from his bag and placed it on the trunk.

"What's in the box?" Shivereen asked.

"Some dreadful little monsters," Grandpa whispered. "They're called **GRINDERS**. They eat up everything in their path, and they don't stop until they're **FULL**!"

THE DREADFUL GRINDERS
COLOR: Bright red
CHARACTERISTICS: Always hungry

Four tiny bugs the size of ants *crawled* out of the box. At first, they didn't move.

Billy leaned in for a closer look. "They're just harmless little insects," he said. "They don't look so dread —"

Before he could finish his sentence, two of the Grinders jumped onto his jacket and began devouring it. The other two began to chow down on the lock. Billy's scream filled the secret room.

"AAAAAAAAAAAAAAAAAAH!"

Then poor Billy fainted once more.

A MYSTERIOUS CLUE

It happened so fast that Creepella and the others couldn't believe their eyes. The **GRINDERS** ate the lock, then the trunk, and then everything that was inside it! Shredded **paper** danced in the air like confetti.

Then all four Grinders began *munching* on Billy's clothes. Once they were done with his jacket sleeves, they moved to his pants. Creepella **shook** Billy, but he didn't wake up.

"Grandpa, they'll **STOP** before they actually **FEAST** on Billy, right?" Shivereen asked nervously.

"Of course!" he replied. "Grinders love **WOOD**, metal, and other material. They don't eat rodents. . . . At least, I think they don't," he added as the Grinders continued to munch and munch.

Poor Billy . . .

Look at those bugs go!

But they stopped eating just a few inches above Billy's ankles. Finally full, they fell asleep.

ZZZZZZZZZZZZZZZZZZZZZZZZZZZZZZZ

"I told you!" Grandpa exclaimed happily. "*Nighty-night*, little ones. You've had enough to eat for today."

Billy SLOWLY opened one eye. "Wh-what happened to me?"

Creepella held out a PAW to help him up. "The dreadful Grinders really liked you," she replied.

"Are they still f-free?" Billy stammered, looking down at his shredded clothes.

"No, they're asleep," she answered. "Unfortunately, they ate everything, including whatever was in that trunk."

"Not everything!" Shivereen exclaimed. "I found a S C R A P of paper!"

Look!

Creepella took it and looked it over.

"Hmm. I can make out two **WORDS**: *Exclusive Resort*," Creepella said.

Shivereen frowned. "That's O D D. There isn't a resort in these mountains."

Before Creepella could comment, her cell phone rang, filling the room with a gloomy sound.

BONG BONG BONG BONG BONG

"Hello?" Creepella answered her phone.

"I figured it out, Creepella. I know what left those pawprints. I'm sure of it! Beyond a **SHADOW** of a doubt!"

"Professor Cleverpaws!" Creepella exclaimed. "That's WONDERFUL news. Please tell me what you know."

"The prints were made by a pair of **stilts**," the professor replied. "A rather old model, actually."

"Hmm, stilts," Creepella said thoughtfully. "Shivereen, write that down!"

DON'T PULL THAT LEVER!

"I'm very puzzled by the stilts," declared Creepella after she hung up the phone.

Grandpa stroked his whiskers. "I was just thinking of a thing. . . ."

"A thing? What THING, Grandpa?" Creepella asked.

"Thing? What thing, dear?" he answered.

"You said you were thinking of a thing," Creepella reminded him.

He nodded. "Yes, of course. Now what was that thing again?"

Creepella sighed. At times, her grandfather was more CONFUSED than a mouse in a maze.

"Don't worry about it," she said. "Let's try to solve this mystery. We haven't found the monsters that are bothering Franco yet."

"Monsters! Of course!" Grandpa said, slapping his paw to his forehead. "We've been in this castle for a while now and I haven't even found the tiniest HINT that a monster is here. Not even a tiny drop of SLIME! Or a shimmering SPLOTCH of ectoplasm!"

"Maybe the MONSTERS clean up after themselves," Shivereen suggested.

"Or maybe what's actually happening —" began Creepella, but a loud "Ouch!" interrupted her.

Everyone turned to look at Billy, who had tripped and fallen FLAT on his back. He got up and looked down to see what had made him lose his BALANCE.

"I tripped on some kind of LEVER," he said, pointing.

"Don't touch it!"

Grandpa Frankenstein yelled.

But it was too late. Billy was curious and had pulled the lever. The floor opened up and a swirling vortex swallowed the entire group.

"Heeeeellllllllp!"
"Heeeeellllllllp!"
"Heeeeellllllllp!"

As he was being hurled through the vortex, Billy tried **DESPERATELY** to hang on to something. His paw grabbed on to Bitewing's foot!

"Hey! Let go of me!" Bitewing screeched.

But it was no use. The vortex carried all five of them through the dark passages of the castle.

Yipeeee!

Let goooooo!

Heeelllp!

DANGERS AND TUNNELS

" AAAAAAAAAAHHH!"

Everyone screamed as the bottom of the vortex opened up and they started to **PLUMMET** through empty space. Then they crashed down — onto a soft velvety cushion.

Poooof!

"What a deliciously **terrifying** flight!" chuckled Grandpa, dusting off his shirt.

"Can we do it again?" asked Shivereen.

"Such a lovely soft landing!" commented Creepella.

But Billy had landed on something pointy. "Th-this is getting dangerous," he said, standing up. "Wh-where are we? And why are we on a mattress?"

"There's nothing dangerous about where we are, Billy-Willy," Creepella assured him. "We happen to be in the castle's CRYPT. And this isn't a mattress — it's a COFFIN!"

Billy quickly jumped out of the coffin — and saw the pointy thing he had landed on. It was a SKULL!

A sk–skull?!

"Well, what do you know? It's **LORD POMODORO FANGLEY'S COFFIN**!" declared Grandpa Frankenstein.

"That's Franco's great-great-grandfather," explained Shivereen. "We saw a painting of him in the Portrait Gallery."

Billy started to **faint**, but Creepella caught him. "No time for that now, Billy-Willy. We're getting closer to solving this **MYSTERY**."

Billy took a deep breath and stepped out of the coffin.

"This is the final resting place of all of Franco's ancestors," said Grandpa. "**Sniff** . . . Such distinguished rodents."

Billy looked around but didn't see an exit. "How d-do we get out of here?"

"We simply need to find the **hidden** door," Grandpa replied. He started to look around.

"Let's see. . . . Ah, yes! Rattle my bones! Here it is!"

Grandpa walked to a STONE sarcophagus leaning against the wall. He pushed on the Fangley family crest carved into it: a **juicy** tomato.

A SMALL DOOR slid open on the bottom of the wall. Grandpa got on his knees and held up Glimmer.

"It's very low. We have to get down on all four paws," he reported.

They *crawled* and *crawled* until they

reached the bottom of a staircase. The stairs seemed to go up and up forever.

"We can do it!" Creepella **cheered**. "Billy-Willy, you keep track of the steps as we climb."

Billy kept count. ". . . two hundred ninety-seven . . . *puff* . . . two ninety-eight, two ninety-nine . . ."

Then Billy **fell** down, exhausted, on the last step — number three hundred.

Creepella picked him up. "Come on, Billy-Willy. We're almost there!"

What an awesome place!

THE OWL TOWER

The stairs opened up to a wide balcony.

"Wh-where are we?" Billy asked, huffing and puffing.

"I believe we're in the OWL TOWER, the HIGHEST point in Castle Marinara," answered Grandpa Frankenstein.

Billy nervously gazed over the railings. The sun was beginning to set, streaking the snowy landscape with shades of pink and gold.

Shivereen happily pointed to landmarks in the distance. "Over there is Gloomeria, and Cacklefur Castle is that way," she said.

"And Squeakspeare Mansion is over there."

I'm so c-cold!

"It's b-beautiful," Billy admitted, shivering. The Grinders had chewed up his warmest clothes. "B-but I'm so c-cold!"

SUDDENLY, Creepella let out a cry. "What's over there in the woods?" she asked, pointing.

Several **TRUCKS** and other construction vehicles were parked among the trees surrounding the castle.

"I had no idea that Franco was thinking of renovating Castle Marinara," Grandpa said, scratching his head.

Creepella squinted into the distance. "There's writing on the sides of the trucks," she said. "But I can't see what it says!"

"No problem!" exclaimed Grandpa. He took another little monster from his bag. "Everyone, meet **Peeper**!"

Creepella picked up the tiny monster. It had two antennae, and at the end of each was a clear **ROUND** lens. She held them in front of her face like **binoculars** and looked at a truck.

"'Stan,'" she read. "'Stan Shadyfur.'"

"Hmm. I've heard that name before," muttered Billy.

Creepella quickly dialed a number on her **CELL PHONE**. "Creepella dear!" exclaimed Boris von Cacklefur at the other end of the line. "How is your **MISSION** going?"

"Very well, Dad," she replied. "I have a question for you.

Have you ever heard of a businessrat named Stan Shadyfur?"

"Of course!" he answered. "He's the one who tried to take Cacklefur Castle away from us last year and turn it into a **spa** resort. He said our murky moat was perfect for relaxing **MUD** baths. He's not a very *honest* rodent, if I do say so."

"Thanks, Dad," Creepella said, hanging up.

"I remember!" exclaimed Billy. "I saw that name in an **ad**!"

"An ad for what?" Creepella asked.

Billy frowned. "I can't remember."

"**CHOCOLATE**-covered mosquitoes?" Bitewing suggested.

"No, I don't think so," Billy said.

"Frightening fashions?" asked Shivereen.
Billy shook his head. "That's not it."

Creepella was getting frustrated. "Rats and
bats! Please concentrate, Billy-Willy. We're
here on a mission, not a vacation."

"That's it!" Billy cried. "A VACATION!
It was an ad for a VACATION in the
snow!"

NOW IT MAKES SENSE!

"Vacation in the snow," Creepella repeated, TAPPING her paw thoughtfully.

As the sky changed from pink to dark blue, Creepella began to pace across the balcony. She started off **slowly** and then walked faster and **faster**.

Then her green **eyes** lit up. "I think I've got it!" she announced. "Shivereen, would you please read your notes?"

Shivereen nodded and began to read out loud.

WHAT FRANCO HAS SEEN/HEARD

- mysterious pranks

- scary shadows

- metallic shrieks

WHAT WE HAVE FOUND IN CASTLE MARINARA

- pawprints made by stilts   - a projector

- a gramophone   - a big sheet

- a scrap of paper with the words

"Exclusive Resort"

- Trucks in the forest nearby with the name

"Stan Shadyfur" on the side. (He's a suspicious

rodent who wanted to turn Cacklefur Castle into

a spa. He is also advertising for vacations in the

snow.)

"Of course! It's clear now!" Creepella exclaimed *triumphantly*.

"Actually, it's getting **DARKER** and **DARKER**," muttered Billy, who was staring at the sky.

"I'm not talking about the sky, Billy-Willy," Creepella said, correcting him. "I'm talking about the ghosts and monsters that are BOTHERING Franco. It all makes sense!"

"**What** makes sense, Auntie?" asked Shivereen impatiently.

"Yes, **what**?" Grandpa Frankenstein asked.

"What what what what what?" shrieked Bitewing as he flapped around them.

"I'll explain it all in a moment," she replied, glancing up at the first stars dotting the sky. "We must hurry and find Franco. It's almost night and he'll be awake soon."

Just as she finished her sentence, a **frightening** shriek echoed throughout the castle.

"AAAAAAAAAAAAAAAHHHHH!"

"What did I tell you?" Creepella said, smiling. "Franco's up — that's the **SHRIEK** a vampire makes when he wakes."

Then a second shriek, more frightening than the first, broke the silence.

"AUUUUUUUUUHHHHH!"

Confused, Grandpa scratched his snout. "Well, rattle my bones! That second sound was **definitely** not Franco!"

SIGN HERE, VAMPIRE!

Franco Fangley had not slept well at all. The bothersome monsters had filled his coffin with **BREAD CRUMBS** again, and he had **tossed** and **turned** all day. Finally, after dozing on and off, he woke up with a shriek as soon as the **MOON** rose.

"I'll go find my friends," Franco muttered out loud. "I wonder if they were

able to discover anything."

Then he heard the loud metallic shriek he heard every night.

"Oh, dear," he said with a yawn. "I hope I'm still dreaming."

Suddenly, the sound of loud organ music filled the room. Then Franco heard a deep, scary voice.

"IT'S NOT A DREEEEEEEEAM!"

"Who said that? And where is that music coming from?" Franco asked, his eyes WIDE with fright.

A tall white ghost suddenly appeared in front of him, towering over him. The specter cast spooky SHADOWS on the walls.

"BE AFRAID, VAMPIRE!"

the ghost howled.

Franco was terrified, but he gathered his courage. He decided to face this unknown ghost once and for all.

"Were you the one who put BREAD CRUMBS in my casket?" Franco asked. "Did you cover the floors with cream cheese? Did you switch my tomato juice bottles with bottles of GARLIC tea?"

The ghost just laughed, and it was a CHILLING sound. Franco SHIVERED and wrapped his cape around his shoulders. But he didn't back down.

"T-tell me once and for all," he said bravely, "wh-what do you want from me?"

"I want you to leave Castle Marinara IMMEDIATELY!" the ghost replied. "If you do not, I will torment you for all ETERNITY!"

"Wh-why should I leave my castle?" Franco

asked. "My family has been living here for centuries!"

"Because I said so!" the ghost thundered menacingly, and Franco trembled with fear. "If you don't, I will **NEVER** leave you in peace. **NEVER!**"

The ghost suddenly produced a sheet of **PAPER** and a *pen*. He handed them to Franco.

Hurry up and sign!

"Before you go, you must sign your name here," the ghost demanded. "Right under where it says '*I give my castle to the ghost who is tormenting me.*'"

Franco was shocked. "I will **NOT** give up my castle!" he insisted.

The ghost came closer.

"It's the only way to get rid of me and go back to your peaceful life," he threatened.

"HURRY UP AND SIGN!"

Franco's paw **trembled** as he held the pen. He did not want to give up his castle. But the ghost terrified him. He felt like he didn't have a choice.

Where are my von Cacklefur friends? he wondered. *I could certainly use some help right now!*

OFF WITH THE SHEET!

Creepella ran down the three hundred steps of the Owl Tower and the rest of the team followed her. When they finally reached Franco's room, an **incredible** sight was before them.

Strange shadows flickered on the walls. Dreary music played. A **GIGANTIC** white ghost hovered over Franco. The vampire held a pen in his shaking paws.

"**STOP!**" Creepella yelled. "Franco, put down that pen!"

The vampire turned around in surprise. Creepella pointed at the ghost.

"You're not fooling me, you **SEWER RAT**!" she shouted.

"Watch what you're saying, you meddling mouse," the ghost said crossly. "I am the **meanest** and most **TERRIFYING** **ghost** in all of Gloomeria!"

The **ghost** floated toward Creepella and the others. As usual, Billy began to **shake** with fright.

Aaargh!

"Creepella, maybe we should just leave Mr. G-ghost alone," Billy suggested.

"Billy-Willy, haven't you figured it out yet? That's not a ghost," she answered.

"It isn't?" Billy asked. "But he's white and FLOATING! And then there are the horrible SHRIEKS and the spooky SHADOWS."

Creepella went to the corner of the room and pulled aside a white cloth.

"This will explain those SHRIEKS and shadows!" she said.

Under the cloth were the gramophone and

Aha!

film projector they had found before.

Creepella turned off both devices. The spooky shadows vanished and the SHRIEKS and dreary music faded.

Then she turned to the ghost. "And now it's your turn, you PHONY PHANTOM!"

Billy tried to stop her. "Don't do it! He could be dangerous!"

But Creepella BRAVELY pulled at the ghost — which was a sheet.

"Off with your DECEITFUL disguise!" Creepella cried.

Everyone gasped. Under the sheet stood a small rodent teetering on top of very tall stilts.

"My dear friends, let me introduce you to the villain in this mystery: Stan Shadyfur!" Creepella announced.

"Stan Shadyfur?" everyone exclaimed.

Franco Fangley dropped the pen in **SURPRISE**. "By my grandpa's fangs! I should have known!" he cried.

"Do you know him?" Creepella asked.

"Of course!" Franco replied. "He's the **DISHONEST** rat who has been trying to get me to give him Castle Marinara for years!"

"And I would have gotten away with it if that **NOSY** mouse hadn't stuck her snout into my business!" Stan yelled, **GLARING** at Creepella. Then he started stomping away on his stilts.

"He's getting away!" Billy yelled.

Grandpa Frankenstein *RAN* to the door, blocking Stan.

"Where do you think you're going, you **FRAUD**?" Grandpa shouted, opening his bag. "Let me introduce you to **Twister**, the

little monster that acts like a rope!"

He twirled the monster in the air like a cowboy using a LASSO. Twister wrapped around Stan so that he couldn't escape.

Grandpa grinned. "And now, my *dearest* granddaughter, please EXPLAIN how you solved this mystery to us!"

Nooo!

Good job, Twister!

A Frightening Finale

"It's simple!" Creepella explained. "Like Franco said, Stan Shadyfur has been trying to buy Castle Marinara. But Franco wouldn't sell. So Stan decided the only way to get the castle was to get rid of its owner!"

"Why did he want the castle?" Billy asked.

"VAMPIRE PEAK is the only place in the entire valley where there is always SNOW," Creepella said. "It's the IDEAL place to build —"

"A SKI RESORT!" exclaimed Shivereen. "That's the 'Exclusive Resort' we found on that scrap of paper."

"Of course!" Billy said, slapping a paw to his forehead. "That's the vacation in the snow he was advertising on that flyer."

"It all makes SENSE," said Grandpa Frankenstein with a nod.

"Thank you so much, my friends!" Franco said GRATEFULLY. "If it weren't for you, I might have lost my castle. This calls for a toast!"

He uncorked a special bottle of tomato juice, which he kept in a **SECRET** spot right next to his coffin.

While everyone was celebrating, Stan Shadyfur unwound himself from Twister and scurried away. Billy spotted him.

"Stan is getting away!" Billy cried.

But the others weren't worried.

"Let him go. He won't come back," Shivereen said with a chuckle.

Creepella still had one question for the **VAMPIRE**. "Franco, when we got here, you were about to sign over your castle to the ghost. Did he really *FRIGHTEN* you that much?"

Franco's pale snout turned as **RED** as tomato juice. "Well, a little," he admitted. "But I was also thinking . . ."

Grandpa patted his shoulder. "Tell us about it, dear friend."

Well...I...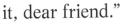

The vampire sighed. "Well, you see, I really **LOVE** Castle Marinara," he began. "It's just that . . . sometimes I feel really **lonely**."

He sadly lowered his head. Everyone was silent for a moment.

Grandpa Frankenstein's eyes lit up. "Who says you have to be alone? I will leave you my BAG OF PESKY LITTLE MONSTERS! They'll keep you company."

"They're adorable little critters," added Shivereen. "You'll see how much FUN you'll have with them!"

"Just make sure you don't wake up the Grinders," Billy muttered under his breath.

PESKY LITTLE MONSTERS

Glimmer
THE LITTLE GLOWING MONSTER

SPECIALTY: Lights up dark places.

FUN FACT: She's afraid of the dark!

THE GRINDERS
THE LITTLE HUNGRY MONSTERS

SPECIALTY: Can quickly and cleanly devour wood, fabric, and other materials.

FUN FACT: The only thing they're afraid of is the dentist!

CHOPPER
THE LITTLE CHOMPING MONSTER

SPECIALTY: Snaps locks and chains in half with his powerful jaws.

FUN FACT: He loves to eat candy!

Peeper
THE LITTLE BINOCULARS MONSTER
SPECIALTY: Lets you look through her lenses to see far away.
FUN FACT: She needs eyeglasses to read!

TWISTER
THE LITTLE ROPELIKE MONSTER
SPECIALTY: Ties things up in very tight knots.
FUN FACT: He knows more than 13,456 types of knots!

Franco smiled. "Would you really leave me the little monsters? That would make me a very happy vampire."

"Of course!" Grandpa Frankenstein replied, hugging his old friend.

Creepella clapped her hands.

"I'M GOING TO WRITE AN AMAZING STORY ABOUT THIS! IT WILL BECOME A BESTSELLER!"

THE END

THE PERFECT PRESENT

Creepella's book became an instant success. I invited Benjamin and Bugsy Wugsy over one night to CELEBRATE with some homemade pizza. Once my cousin Trap heard about the pizza, he came over, too. While I made appetizers with my nephew and his friend, Trap searched my refrigerator for the perfect pizza toppings.

"How about clams, grape jelly, mayonnaise, and a squirt of whipped cream?" Trap suggested.

I shook my head in disgust. "Absolutely not!"

"You're right," Trap said, nodding. "We need to add some HOT SAUCE."

"No way, Trap," I protested.

"What if we add a few PICKLES?" Trap asked.

I sighed. "The secret to a good pizza is to keep it simple."

"I agree, Uncle," said Benjamin. "In fact, the king of pizzas is the cheese pizza."

"Exactly," Bugsy Wugsy agreed. "Just tomato sauce and mozzarella."

I smacked my paw on my forehead. "Holey cheese! That's what I forgot. The tomato sauce!"

At that moment, the window opened and a purple bat came flapping in. It was Bitewing! He was carrying a mysterious BOTTLE in his claws.

"I've brought you a gift from CREEPELLA

VON CACKLEFUR," he announced. "It's a bottle of tomato sauce from Castle Marinara!"

Lucky us! Creepella had saved our dinner with the perfect present!

The **pizzas** we made were truly **delicious** — except for the one we gave to Bitewing. He wanted his topped with mosquito jelly!

Yummy!

Bon appétit!

If you liked this book, be sure to check out my next adventure!

FRIGHT NIGHT

It's time for Mysterious Valley's most anticipated competition of the year! The mouse who performs the best rhymes for the public and judges will be crowned Greatest Poet. Creepella's father, Boris von Cacklefur, has a secret weapon for the championship this year — he's going to improvise a rap . . . of fear!

And don't miss any of my other fabumouse adventures!

#1 Lost Treasure of the Emerald Eye

#2 The Curse of the Cheese Pyramid

#3 Cat and Mouse in a Haunted House

#4 I'm Too Fond of My Fur!

#5 Four Mice Deep in the Jungle

#6 Paws Off, Cheddarface!

#7 Red Pizzas for a Blue Count

#8 Attack of the Bandit Cats

#9 A Fabumouse Vacation for Geronimo

#10 All Because of a Cup of Coffee

#11 It's Halloween, You 'Fraidy Mouse!

#12 Merry Christmas, Geronimo!

#13 The Phantom of the Subway

#14 The Temple of the Ruby of Fire

#15 The Mona Mousa Code

#16 A Cheese-Colored Camper

#17 Watch Your Whiskers, Stilton!

#18 Shipwreck on the Pirate Islands

#19 My Name Is Stilton, Geronimo Stilton

#20 Surf's Up, Geronimo!

#21 The Wild, Wild West

#22 The Secret of Cacklefur Castle

A Christmas Tale

#23 Valentine's Day Disaster

#24 Field Trip to Niagara Falls

#25 The Search for Sunken Treasure

#26 The Mummy with No Name

#27 The Christmas Toy Factory

#28 Wedding Crasher

#29 Down and Out Down Under

#30 The Mouse Island Marathon

#31 The Mysterious Cheese Thief

Christmas Catastrophe

#32 Valley of the Giant Skeletons

#33 Geronimo and the Gold Medal Mystery

#34 Geronimo Stilton, Secret Agent

#35 A Very Merry Christmas

#36 Geronimo's Valentine

#37 The Race Across America

#38 A Fabumouse School Adventure

#39 Singing Sensation

#40 The Karate Mouse

#41 Mighty Mount Kilimanjaro

#42 The Peculiar Pumpkin Thief

#43 I'm Not a Supermouse!

#44 The Giant Diamond Robbery

#45 Save the White Whale!

#46 The Haunted Castle

#47 Run for the Hills, Geronimo!

#48 The Mystery in Venice

#49 The Way of the Samurai

#50 This Hotel is Haunted!

And coming soon!

#51 The Enormouse Pearl Heist

1. Mountains of the Mangy Yeti
2. Cacklefur Castle
3. Angry Walnut Tree
4. Rattenbaum Mansion
5. Rancidrat River
6. Bridge of Shaky Steps
7. Squeakspeare Mansion
8. Slimy Swamp
9. Ogre Highway
10. Gloomeria
11. Shivery Arts Academy
12. Horrorwood Studios

MYSTERIOUS VALLEY

DEAR MOUSE FRIENDS, GOOD-BYE UNTIL THE NEXT BOOK!

CACKLEFUR CASTLE

1. Oozing moat

2. Drawbridge

3. Grand entrance

4. Moldy basement

5. Patio, with a view of the moat

6. Dusty library

7. Room for unwanted guests

8. Mummy room

9. Watchtower

10. Creaking staircase

11. Banquet room

12. Garage (for antique hearses)

13. Bewitched tower

14. Garden of carnivorous plants

15. Stinky kitchen

16. Crocodile pool and piranha tank

17. Creepella's room

18. Tower of musky tarantulas

19. Bitewing's tower (with antique contraptions)

No part of this book may be reproduced, stored in a retrieval system, or transmitted in any form or by any means, electronic, mechanical, photocopying, recording, or otherwise, without written permission of the copyright holder. For information regarding permission, please contact: Atlantyca S.p.A., Via Leopardi 8, 20123 Milan, Italy; e-mail foreignrights@atlantyca.it, www.atlantyca.com.

ISBN 978-0-545-39348-5

Copyright © 2011 by Edizioni Piemme S.p.A., Via Tiziano 32, 20145 Milan, Italy.

International Rights © Atlantyca S.p.A.

English translation © 2012 by Atlantyca S.p.A.

GERONIMO STILTON names, characters, and related indicia are copyright, trademark, and exclusive license of Atlantyca S.p.A. All rights reserved. The moral right of the author has been asserted.

Based on an original idea by Elisabetta Dami.
www.geronimostilton.com

Published by Scholastic Inc., 557 Broadway, New York, NY 10012. SCHOLASTIC and associated logos are trademarks and/or registered trademarks of Scholastic Inc.

Stilton is the name of a famous English cheese. It is a registered trademark of the Stilton Cheese Makers' Association. For more information, go to www.stiltoncheese.com.

Text by Geronimo Stilton
Original title *Un vampiro da salvare!*
Cover by Giuseppe Ferrario (pencils and inks) and
Giulia Zaffaroni (color)
Illustrations by Ivan Bigarella (pencils and inks) and
Daria Cerchi (color)
Graphics by Yuko Egusa

Special thanks to Tracey West
Translated by Lidia Morson Tramontozzi
Interior design by Elizabeth Frances Herzog

12 11 10 9 8 7 6 5 4 3 2 1   12 13 14 15 16 17/0

Printed in the U.S.A.   40

First printing, August 2012

Geronimo Stilton

CREEPELLA VON CACKLEFUR
RETURN OF THE VAMPIRE

W9-AZD-914

Scholastic Inc.

New York   Toronto   London   Auckland

Sydney   Mexico City   New Delhi   Hong Kong